SEDUCTIVE

SEDUCTIVE

Seductive

W. Winters

He's forbidden, dangerous, and everything that's bad for me. More than that, the life he leads is exactly why I'd been on the run.

The seductive and powerful air around him is what drew me in, the reminder of what could have and should have been years ago.

His dark gaze riddled with desire could always see through me. Deep down to the core of what I craved most. *To be his.*

And so I agreed. I came back. I chose him even when I knew I shouldn't.

If only it were so easy to forget the past. If only our

mistakes didn't hold on to us, harder and more violently than we could hold on to each other.

Seductive is an extension of Addison and Daniel's story, *Possessive*. Although it can be read on its own, it's recommended you start with *Possessive*.

I knew when I came back here that I was making a choice. I was choosing Daniel over everything. Over the life I'd live without him and where I'd live it — far away from here and these memories.

Men like him come with those kinds of complications.

Men like him are… There are many words I could use to describe him. The most fundamental statement, though, is so easily admitted and it's the very reason I chose him.

Men like him need to be loved or the damage will consume them. More than anything. In this cruel world he's cemented into, with a tragic past and ruthless tasks ahead, he needed to be loved. He still does…

My gaze lingers on what looks like carrots or sweet potatoes, some sort of orange mush in tiny little glass jars. The packs are stacked high on the shelf. The black and white silhouette of a smiling baby stares back at me and I have to push my cart forward, listening to the quiet squeaks of the turning wheels as I think about how I ended up here.

I was reckless, that's how.

Grocery shopping with Daniel wasn't one of the things I was considering when I returned to where I grew up. I was thinking of the drugs, the violence, his brothers, and how powerful they've become. It wasn't like this back then. Not at all. It wasn't this bad. Back then, I thought they'd grow out of it one day. At least that's what I'd hoped. I didn't think they'd eventually come to rule this merciless world.

It's all surreal. Every day since I've been back has brought a fear and tension that's seeping into my every waking moment.

He knows. That's why I'm here.

Shopping for milk and orange juice feels like a sham. Like for a moment, I can maybe pretend this past week didn't happen. As if the white noise from the man on the intercom can drown out the sounds of the last six months.

"Feel like you're playing house, now?" Daniel quips as I stop and watch him settle a jar of salsa, two bags of tortillas, and a case of something else into the half-full cart. His tone is optimistic.

"I didn't say 'playing house,'" I correct him and note how cold it feels along with how dull my heart beats.

I wish I could fix my face right now; I wish I could smile and pretend like it's all fine, like they all do, but it's not and I'm finding it difficult to hide it from him. Especially after what just happened. I could deal with it; I was dealing with it. But things change. And the past month changed everything.

He doesn't hide a damn thing from me anymore, so it'd be unfair to hide from him. But what's left for him to see isn't what I want to be there.

I'm still staring blankly at the case beneath the bags of chips when his muscular forearm cuts off my vision. His strong hand wraps over mine on the handle of the cart and his other grips my chin, lifting it up. I have to look away from his rolled-up sleeve and into his dark eyes. With his rough stubble in need of a shave, and his hair messy on top, he looks as rough as I feel. Rough looks damn sexy on Daniel Cross though. It always has; it's who he's meant to be.

"I know it's been hard," he says, and his voice is low and calm, his gaze soft and comforting.

"Hard?" I force a smile to my lips as the bottom one wobbles and he looks past me, dropping his grip on my chin. I'm quick to reach out and take his hand though. I just need to feel him. "I'm sorry," I tell him quickly. That's what I am: sorry, pathetic, weak. The list goes on. I knew what he had become. What *they* had become. And I still chose to come back. I did this. It was my fault. But a lie slips out instead. It's easier to deal with it if I lie to myself the way he lies to me. "I didn't know what I was coming back to and it's been…"

"Hard," he answers for me.

"Stressful," I correct him and the tension grows tenfold between us. I look up to my right when I notice motionless figures and feel their eyes on us. My own are pricking, distraught from what's happened and how much I'm losing.

I can hear the harsh swallow Daniel makes and I watch the cords in his neck tighten as he holds my hand in his. He lifts my hand to his lips and then kisses my knuckles. One by one.

"It'll be okay," he whispers against my skin, and all the warmth from those words travels through me, calming me. Making me feel lighter, as if I believe him wholeheartedly.

It doesn't change what happened.

Nothing can ever change what happened, but we have a choice about how we handle it. I'm starting to think I made the wrong one.

That's why I hold his hand longer than he holds mine. That's why I stand there watching him leave when he tells me he's getting the rest of what's on the list and says for me to just get the bread. I don't miss the depth in his eyes, the distance that lingers. Every day, he's farther away from me. He knows. He can feel it too. It's like the slow unraveling of thick twine. It's obvious and torturous to watch.

It wasn't this way when we were just teenagers. It wasn't like this at all.

The power he and his brothers now have comes with violence I've never seen before and a harshness that's required to survive. Shopping for fucking groceries is his way of showing me it's normal, it's okay, that life is more than that brutal side of the Cross brothers and what they do.

I can't look past the darkness though. It's never going to feel "okay." This sense of danger that lingers in my blood is always going to be there.

I have to find my place with it. That's not something he can help me with. I have tried. I thought I was there. I was wrong.

It's caused damage I can't take back. That's what hurts the most. I can't take this last month back.

"You all right?" A deep baritone voice from behind me startles me. With a quick intake of breath and my hand reaching up to my rapidly beating heart, I turn around to see a man standing there. He's older, maybe in his late forties. Kind eyes with gentle lines surrounding them meet mine.

It takes me a moment to realize when he arches his brow that he's waiting for my response.

With a few blinks to bring my mind back to the present and a shake of my head, I tell him, "Fine, sorry."

I push my cart forward thinking I'm blocking his path, but he doesn't have a cart and he doesn't seem to have any intention to move either. His boot-clad feet are firmly planted and my eyes move from them, up his dark-wash jeans and button-down white shirt to his questioning gaze.

"I'm fine." My voice is stern and carries a harshness I don't like to use with strangers when I repeat myself; this guy needs to stay the hell out of my business.

When he crosses his arms, I can tell he has some muscle to him. The cotton fabric tightens around his biceps, just as my hands do on the handle of the cart. There's an air to him that changes, a knowingness about him that sends a chill down my spine.

It's a look I recognize. It's a look I don't like. The type of look that makes me want to run.

"I don't think you are fine," he challenges and the bitterness of having this man judge me creeps into the snide response I'm ready to spit out at him. He continues, stopping my words and any breath I was daring to take. "I know he's a murderer. I know he killed your foster father. And it looks like you're having a difficult time dealing with things… just from my perspective, Miss Fawn."

That prick that has crawled slowly down my spine flows over my body in a single wave, nearly buckling my knees. I can feel the color drain from my face. Slowly, just like the twine fraying and unraveling. I don't know who this man is, but I know damn well I shouldn't be talking to him.

I have to concentrate on keeping my breathing steady — in and out — and focus on not reacting.

Murderer.

My foster father.

Daniel didn't kill him.

My eyes dart to the man and I try to hold his prying gaze.

My head wants to shake just slightly, it wants to deny what he's saying, but it can't. I can't react. I can't show him a damn thing.

Daniel didn't murder him though. That happened years ago. Before I ever even thought of leaving this place, before everything else happened. I want to speak the words, the need to defend Daniel pushing the words toward the tip of my tongue.

I bite down on the inside of my cheek instead, screaming in my head to stay silent. But silence brings questions. Not just mine but also this man's.

I've never questioned my foster father's death. It was a burglary. That's what the news said.

The Cross brothers are good at covering things up. I've heard and seen things though. Especially recently.

I know what Daniel's capable of and what he'll do out of anger. I know he loved me back then. What my foster father did… That's the second reason I stay bitterly quiet, even as the questions choke me. I hate even thinking of that man. I was only a child and he was a predator. I'd rather spit on his gravestone than mention his name.

The third reason I keep biting the inside of my cheek until I taste a tinge of blood is the most important. The man who stands silent in front of me knows more than I do. I may be the sorry excuse for a woman Daniel's chosen to be his wife, but I'm not stupid. I'm smart enough to know when to keep my mouth shut. So I do. I stand there, waiting to see if a threat comes.

Near silence reigns with only the steady hum of the coolers behind us as I stare back at him.

After a moment, his lips kick up into an asymmetric smile. "Did you not know?" he questions but doesn't wait for a response. "Maybe you didn't know then, but you know now." His eyes narrow as he nods, persuading me to believe him.

"Who are you?" It's the first question I imagine Daniel asking when I tell him what happened.

"Cody Walsh. Your boyfriend knows who I am."

"Fiancé," I correct him.

His forehead scrunches when he stares down at my hand, the one lacking a ring, and subconsciously, my thumb runs over my ring finger.

"Congratulations," he comments. His demeanor has completely changed with every passing minute that he scrutinizes me, trying to determine where my place is in this world.

Truth be told, I have no idea what he'll find; I'm still trying to figure that out myself.

"Addison Fawn … soon-to-be Addison Cross," he says but doesn't infuse any type of emotion into the statement. It's only matter-of-fact. "Any relation to Bethany Fawn?"

Confusion travels over my face as I try to recall a Bethany of any sort.

"Oh, you don't know that either? She's the woman Jase, your fiancé's brother, has been seeing." Again, I don't answer, and I try to keep from giving him any response in my expression. He only smirks as he walks past me, letting me know to tell Daniel he said hi.

"Will do," I manage to bite out without an ounce of resentment as I accept his challenge.

I didn't know Daniel's brother was seeing anyone. I sure as hell don't know a Bethany *Fawn*. Apparently, I don't know a lot of things.

What I do know is already destroying me.

A hint of lemon in the wood polish invades my lungs as I breathe in deep, gripping the armrests of the wingback chair.

I can't look at my brothers, neither of them. I'm breaking down. The farther away Addison is, the worse I crumble. If they look too closely, if I speak too loudly, they'll see every fucking crack.

Too bad I can't help myself during this bitch of a conversation.

"We have a soft truce." Carter's voice is calm, but he knows my reaction will be anything but.

"Fuck that," I say, letting the darkly spoken words fall without looking at either him or Jase. I stare past my brother and into the woods that line the property through the paned window behind him. The shades of green blur as my blood heats with anger.

"He stays out of our way and we give him details. That was the truce." Carter speaks in time with the tapping of the pen in his hand on the desk.

"Going up to Addison and scaring her isn't exactly staying out of our way."

"He scared her?" he questions me and I don't have time to push out the snide remark: *How the fuck else should she feel?*

"Maybe we pissed him off with the last deal? We didn't exactly keep our word," Jase says carefully, and I can feel him watching me, gauging my reaction with every syllable, but I use everything in me to stay still and not give them any more than I already have.

Leaning forward, my throat is dry as I speak clearly to both of them. "He walked up to my soon-to-be wife. He tried to get to her, to get in her head." My back hits the chair as I force myself to stay seated and not turn over every piece of furniture in my brother's office. "He left like a coward before I could get my hands on him. I want his fucking head!" My pulse races as I lose control with the last sentence.

We own this town. We own the cops.

Cody Walsh is supposed to be easy. He's supposed to be predictable. All that went to shit last month. Just like everything else.

Carter ignores me, or at least he ignores my anger to instead direct his comments to Jase. "If Walsh is pissed about what we did, he'll get over it. We do what we have to." Facing me and hardening his voice, he asks me, "What exactly did he say to her?"

"That we killed that prick. That he knows I'm a murderer and he knows she's not okay."

"That's how he said it?"

Carter's constant questioning makes me inhale sharply as I straighten my shoulders and stare him down, not giving him a single word in response. Not trusting myself to speak.

"He still needs us." Carter speaks first.

"And we still need him," Jase reminds us all. It's his ass on the line. This is all his fault. His sloppy choices made us take the deal with Walsh.

Although Carter's talking to Jase, the statement is directed at me. "Until we find the footage he's black-mailing you with, his head stays on."

My blunt nails tap along the polished wood in a soothing rhythm, so at odds with what I feel. "And what am I supposed to do in the meantime? Let him scare her? Let him get to her?"

"No," both Jase and Carter say at the same time. My eyes dart between the two of them, judging their response for sincerity until I can nod.

With my thumb brushing against the fleshy tips of my fingers, I ask Carter, my older brother and the one I rely on in order to move forward every day in this shit of a mess we've gotten ourselves into with a dirty cop, "What can I do?" I feel weak asking them rather than acting. I hate this and I know they can feel the turmoil rolling off of me in waves as I close my eyes and try to loosen my tight throat. "I need something to give her. Something to make all this better." *There's nothing to make it better*, a voice hisses inside my head and I lean forward, burying my face in my hands. I grit out the words between my clenched teeth as I add, "I fucking hate this."

"For now, I'll remind Walsh that our women will be respected and they stay out of it—"

"She said…" I have to swallow the hard lump in my throat before continuing as I stare past him again at the ambers and emeralds of the trees. "She said he seemed concerned, then he was… gauging her. He's trying to flip her."

"Concerned?"

"She isn't handling the recent events well." I can barely get out the words. Each syllable claws the back of my throat before it's spoken. "He approached her, she said, because she didn't look like she was doing well."

The leather behind Carter groans and protests as he readjusts in his chair opposite the desk from me.

"If he thinks she's a weak spot, he's wrong," I tell him and there's more defensiveness in my cadence than I wanted. "She would never tell anyone anything."

"No one thinks she would."

"That's why he brought up the foster fuck? You think he was gauging her to see if it was true? To see if she knows anything?" Jase asks.

"That's what she thinks," I answer him. "If he's trying to get more dirt on us, we need to end this now. Finish him."

"He can't know for sure about her foster father, how many fucking years ago was it? And Addison would never give anything up."

"How did he know?" I question them. It happened a decade ago. No one ever knew. It was only us.

"Forensics, maybe evidence." Jase sounds suspicious but shakes his head at the thought and shrugs as he adds, "Maybe word on the street, but I don't see how."

"He's bluffing. He had a hunch and he's testing us to see if we'll play into his hands."

It's quiet as the information is digested. This balancing act is getting harder and harder. What was once planks of wood feels like a thin tightrope now.

Carter takes a deep inhale before speaking. "Let's make him feel comfortable. That's the only way we can use him until we're safe to get rid of him."

Make him feel comfortable... I'm seething inside. This isn't the way things used to be. It's complicated and every move we make only gets us deeper and deeper into bed with the devil.

"Did you tell Addison about her father—" Carter starts to ask, but stops and corrects himself. "Foster father?"

I simply nod before replying, "Last night when she told me."

I remember the way she couldn't look me in the

eyes before I told her. The way she turned her back to me to go to the bathroom. The way her knuckles turned white as she stood there gripping the doorknob, not moving but not asking. She wanted to know, but she knows better than to ask. That's what we decided. I tell if she asks, but she never asks. She doesn't want to know. "I told her because I thought she'd want to know the truth."

"It's been years."

"A decade."

"She never even considered it was us back then." I repeat my thoughts, but out loud now. "No one did."

"What did she say?" Jase questions, concern clearly written on his face.

The vision returns to me of her eyes closing slowly, her chin dropping as she took in a shuddering breath. Her response came out as nothing but a whisper and then she closed the door to the bathroom, leaving me sitting there, watching the glass knob and wishing it had been my hand she was holding when I confessed.

"She said, 'thank you,'" I tell them.

"Do you think she gave anything away to Walsh?"

"No," I say and my answer is hard as I glare at Jase. He stares back, unmoving, but there's sympathy in his expression.

"He can't prove anything," Carter says between us, cutting through the thinly veiled tension.

"Since when do we let someone make us feel threatened?"

"Since he has evidence that will put me away for life," Jase answers me. "We tread carefully until Declan can find something on him and get rid of every shred of proof Walsh has."

"He's digging into everything he can so we'll work with him," Carter says, then clears his throat and sits back farther in his chair. "I'll send him a message, letting him know not to go near Addison and that his concern is unwarranted."

"A message?"

"It's the safe—"

Anger forces me to rise from my seat. "A fucking message?"

"Calm down."

"You aren't the one who lost a baby! I lost my child." The strength in my voice is all but forgotten as I voice it for the first time. They already know, but I haven't said it yet. I haven't had the audacity to breathe that truth to life. "Your wife is still pregnant. Mine isn't." Everything cracks. The air, my voice, my damn insides shatter to brittle shards.

They sit there in silence as I slowly retake my seat. *Just breathe. Calm down.* How can I do either when everything is falling apart?

Jase's firm hand squeezes my forearm as he tells me, "I know it's difficult on her; we need to keep her safe and protected."

"It was stress. That's what the doctor said. She lost

the baby and this bullshit isn't stopping. It's getting worse."

All that surrounds me is silence. All that lingers inside of me is guilt. I don't know how to fix this, and I don't think anyone else knows either.

"She isn't supposed to know anything. That was our deal. But she sees how tense everyone is. She knows how much danger we've been in. She's witnessed shit firsthand… I don't think she can handle this. She wasn't supposed to know any details. That's what she wanted." The admission flows from me like a Catholic at church. Safe in the confessional, waiting to hear my penance, praying for it all to be okay. *Just tell me what to do to make it all right.*

"Maybe that's the problem," Carter suggests, and I lift my blurred gaze to his dark one.

"What?" At least my question is presentable.

"Maybe she should know," Jase says before Carter. "Maybe if she knew details, she'd feel like she has more control. Control is a damn good way to deal with stress. Even if it's only in details and not action."

I don't have time to answer; a knock at the door interrupts the conversation. It's a soft rap, quick but firm.

Before Carter can tell whoever it is to come in, the heavy door creaks open, bringing with it the light from the hall, and Addison's shadow spills into the room before she does. Her hand stays on the edge of the door when she asks, "Is it all right if I come in?"

My brothers don't answer for me, but I nod once.

The room's so quiet I can practically hear her swallow as she steps into it, not shutting the door for privacy. "I just remembered something. Something I didn't tell you." Our eyes lock as she wrings her fingers around one another. Her hair's still damp from the shower, making it look darker than her dirty-blonde should be. Her lack of sleep is just as evident. Still, she's beautiful.

She clears her throat, staring at the intricately woven rug beneath the desk and stopping a small distance from me in her bare feet.

Her small form clothed in loose pajamas is at odds with the three of us. She belongs here though. She is my counterpart in every way. I only wish I didn't hurt her like I do.

"He brought up my last name," she finally says clearly. Her admission makes a deep crease settle in my forehead.

"Fawn?" I question and that gets Jase's attention.

She nods, glancing between Jase and me. "He asked if I was related to Bethany." She speaks directly to Jase as if he'd have an answer, but he wears the same expression I do.

"I never really knew my family, so… I don't know." The insecurity in her tone is undeniable, as is her curiosity.

"You should ask her," Jase comments. "We can have dinner tomorrow night."

"That would be good for us," Carter agrees. "I'll ask Aria if she's up for cooking." All the while I stare at Addison, waiting for her to give me some sign that she's all right.

Anything. I need something from her.

"I'll ask her," Addison quickly speaks up, then adds, "I'd like to talk to her anyway." A weak smile lingers on her lips as my brothers nod in agreement. It's quiet for a moment and I can see the questions in her eyes.

"Anything else?" I prod.

"Were you talking about Walsh?"

My brothers stay quiet. They handle their relationships the way they want and I do the same. I seem to be the only one failing though. "Do you want in on the details?" I always ask. She knows when something's wrong, when I'm worried. When things have gone to shit. I'd never make her an accessory, but I'll give her what I can if she wants it.

"No," she answers, and her smile turns tight, forming a straight line before she drops her hands to her sides and says she'll head out to talk to Aria.

"How are you doing, Addie?" Jase asks her before she can leave.

"Better. I think I just needed a hot shower." Time passes with a click of the clock, a second that waits for what else is on her mind. A piece of me is dying to scream for her to speak up. To ask. The piece that wants to tell her everything. The other part of me, the bigger part, wants to shield her.

She leaves as quickly as she came, which is probably for the best.

The less she knows, the less stress she'll have. She doesn't need to worry about this shit. It's our mess. Not hers.

I need to fix this. I just don't know how.

Cody Walsh. A million questions linger in my mind after looking up his name online all last night. More questions scream in my head when I think about what Daniel confessed. They killed a man years ago who deserved to be hurt. They killed him because of what he did to me. They *killed* him.

How many moments have gone by where I've mentioned my childhood in passing? Or lack thereof, rather. We talked about how I was in home after home. When we found out I was pregnant, it was all I could think about. All I could talk about.

I was worried I wouldn't know how to be a good mother, because I never had one. It opened the floodgates for all those memories. When I was young, I didn't even think I'd ever be able to get pregnant. Just the thought makes my stomach churn; it's because of what he did to me. The doctors said the scar tissue on

my cervix could make it harder to open. I had problems and complications. All the aftermath of the man
who was supposed to take care of me.

I brought it up maybe three or four times in the last
two months when we found out I was pregnant. I
couldn't *not* talk about it. No matter how much I hate
to go back to those times in my life.

Daniel had so many opportunities to tell me, but he
never did.

I never asked, but how would I have even known to
question it? Fear has been replaced by something else.
Something larger than it. A dying need to know.

"Hey." Aria's tone is already consoling when she
greets me, ripping me from my thoughts as I place the
heavy porcelain plates on the counter.

I didn't expect to feel this way toward her. There's a
gap between us now, when only weeks ago, nothing
separated us. Now I'm careful with what I say and how
I say it. I'm careful I don't put this sadness on her. Just
like she's careful with me now.

"How's it going?" she asks.

I can hear the emotions in her voice just as easily as
the clank of the dishes. The sympathy, the guilt I know
she feels because she's still pregnant when I'm not. She
and Chloe, Sebastian's wife, are carrying so well.
Glowing is the correct term. And then there's me, dull
with a forced smile as I turn to her, leaning the small of
my back against the granite counter.

"Hey, yourself," I answer her with enough pep in my

voice to lighten the tension. I don't want anyone to feel sorry for me. It's life. It's death. It's whatever fate has in store. I don't want her to look at me and feel pity. I'd rather she look at me and see how happy I am for her.

That's one shining light in all this darkness.

"We're cooking for everyone tonight, if you're up for that?" I ask her.

"Family dinner tonight?" Aria eyes me curiously as one perfectly plucked eyebrow arches. She knows something's up, but she doesn't ask. She used to always ask.

"Does that mean something's going on?" Chloe asks as she enters, the faint sound of bags rustling carrying through the kitchen with her. Her husband is best friends with Carter and his right-hand man, but she doesn't live in the main house of the estate like the rest of us. She and Sebastian have a place deeper in the woods; it's still protected though. At first, I thought it was sweet for all of us to live so close. But the more I think about it, the fact that we need to be protected, the more it startles me.

I watch as she sets a large brown paper bag down on the table, her belly protruding, round and an obvious sign that she's in her second trimester.

Taking off her light jacket, she lays it across the chair and then smooths her flowing cream blouse down her front.

"Carter told Sebastian and he told me," Chloe says, answering the unspoken question. "I brought everything for cheesecake," she adds easily with a genuine smile. She doesn't look at me like I'm broken, but that's because she doesn't know me well. She doesn't see how off I am like Aria does. She can't tell that I'm damaged goods because she doesn't know what I was like before. It's comforting, really.

"So?" she questions. "Is something going on?"

"What do you mean?" I have no idea what she's referring to. "Something is always going on."

"Well, have you guys been doing family dinners where this is normal, or is this a way for the guys to keep us in line?"

"I never thought about it like that." The murmured words are accompanied by a deep line settling into my forehead as I consider it.

"If something's up, Bastian better tell me," Chloe comments as she unloads the contents of her bag on the table.

"No, nothing's up. It's a little tense right now. But no more than usual. The only thing eating at Carter is a cop who's getting to Jase. He caused a little stir yesterday."

"How do you know for sure?" I ask her.

"Carter keeps me updated. We have a little ritual. It calms him and keeps his head clear to talk things out."

"I can't imagine how that could be calming." I don't realize I've spoken until the words are out there and the room goes quiet.

Chloe's huff is amused when I look at her with wide

eyes. "You'd be surprised how much a conversation is worth." Her gaze falls for just a moment, but I see it happen. The haze of a smile falls along with it. "How have you been?"

Aria's been popping grapes in her mouth, but she pauses when Chloe ventures into *that* territory. Her bump isn't so visible. Our babies would have been about a month apart.

It's hard to contain the deluge of emotions.

"You can say it sucks. Or that it hurts. Or that you're better or worse… You can tell me to shut my mouth too and mind my own damn business," she offers after rattling off a list of appropriate responses.

I feel like it's my fault. Like I should have known better. I say the words in my head, because I can't admit them. Not to Aria and Chloe. Not to Daniel. I don't even want to know that's how I feel. But I do.

"We should make dinner," I suggest in a whisper. "Just because I'm suffering a loss doesn't mean I can't be happy for all we have," I add and Chloe gives me a small smile that doesn't reach her eyes.

"The dinner for the non-worrying mob wives," Chloe jokes.

"We are not the mob." Aria hisses the admonishment before eating another grape. "It's been hectic and there's always something to worry about, but—"

I don't want the tears to fall, but I can't hide them. My face is hot and my breath comes in short pants. The next inhale is harsh, and with it, both women come to me. "I'm sorry," I say, and my words are strangled as I rush past them for a napkin on the table so I can stop it all.

"Don't say that. Don't be sorry for crying. I've always thought that was the silliest of things."

"It's good to cry." Aria's voice is so soothing. She is my rock in all of this. She's steady and we share so much in common. She grew up in this life though. She didn't run away from it all. "Sometimes crying — showing mourning, showing vulnerability — leads to the best things."

I respond with the one truth the last six months has taught me and say, "You can't be vulnerable in this world."

She counters my statement as I swipe the napkin under my eyes, drying them, calming my breathing and feeling foolish all over again.

"Of course you can," Aria corrects me. "We all are. Trying to hide that isn't going to fool anyone." She emphasizes, "We're all vulnerable."

All I have in response is a sniffle and then I rest my head on her shoulder. "I didn't mean to cry though; I don't want you to think seeing you guys makes me sad." I can barely get the statement out, because it's not entirely true. Still, I don't want them to think it.

We hide truths like that, don't we?

"So, weird thing," I blurt out, cutting off Chloe, who no doubt has something sweet to say, and instead I help her move all the items on the table to the counter as I speak. It's back to business, back to cooking for this non-worrying dinner. "Did you know Jase has a girl-friend?" I ask them and my tone is so much peppier than I feel. I heard once though, if you speak like you're happy, you'll start to feel like it.

"Carter told me a couple of days ago. She's funny but with a dry sense of humor and she's very blunt."

"Sounds delightful," Chloe jokes.

"She's also coming to dinner, I think."

Aria eyes me before grabbing a large bowl from the lower cabinet and I take that as my cue to unwrap Chloe's cream cheese.

Looks like the dessert will be done before the actual meal at this rate.

"Bastian also mentioned she's a nurse. Should be good to have one of those in the family."

"Family," Aria says and rolls her eyes.

"I didn't mean in a mob way."

"Her last name is Fawn," I comment to no one in particular and unwrap the next bar of cream cheese. "I wonder if she knows if we're related."

"Like biologically? Or from… Is your last name your mother's or did you get that from a…?" Aria stops mid-thought and it's then that I realize from the look on her face that she was going to say *foster family* but stopped herself because she thought it would hurt me to hear it. She stopped herself because she knows about the fresh wounds.

She knows because Carter told her.

Or maybe she's known since I came back. I wonder if Carter told her everything all the way back then.

"You know I still love you, right?" I question Aria and quickly add, "And that I'm happy for you, both of you?" I look between them both, hoping they know it's true. I may be held together by glue and tape and questioning my decisions, but I know I'm happy for them.

"I know," Aria answers with kind eyes. She repeats, "I know."

DANIEL

Tyler always hid it from her. He was good at it though.

Tyler's all I can think about as we sit down at the table. Three brothers and a friend. One brother late, as per usual. Another never coming to a family dinner again.

He didn't have this problem with Addison. He was good at hiding it. He hid so much from her; I just don't know how he could do it.

"The candles are a nice touch," Addison says and smiles warmly at Aria, who does a small curtsy and the three girls let out a peal of feminine laughter.

Addison's is short, genuine. But it disappears quickly. It's like the warm water of the ocean, splashing on the tips of your toes before retreating all too soon. I miss it already. I find myself staying still, wanting it to come back.

The day must've gone well for her. With a glass of wine in her hand and a beautiful flush in her cheeks, she's unwinding with the help of the alcohol.

"Just let me smell one more time," Aria says and inhales close to the large goblet at the same time Carter wraps his arm around her waist and pulls her into his lap. Another wave of giggling leaves the women and then is replaced by soft hums as the other two women are kissed and kiss back, falling into their seats for dinner.

Mine's already seated, and when I look to her, her lips are on the wineglass. So instead of kissing her, I place my hand over hers on her lap. My fingers slip into the spaces between hers, feeling her soft skin, her warmth. Before she places the glass back on the table, her fingers close around mine, bringing them closer together, and she doesn't let go. Not until the large bowl of antipasto salad is passed.

"Looks delicious, ladies." Sebastian's compliment is rewarded with a story from Aria about how she learned a new recipe for the main dish.

Lasagna, candlelight, and delicate dishes, the hum of chatter and constant smiles. Everything in the room is full of life, but that's not how I feel. It's not the reality I'm living in.

If Tyler were here though, he'd fit right in, and that would help Addison. He was good at hiding. He would have been good for her.

I wash the thought away with a single swig of the

bourbon in front of me. I try to tell myself he's on my mind because of what happened recently. And not because I truly think Addison would be better off if he were still here.

It's not like before. Nothing is. I have to remind myself of that sometimes. The memories of what used to be, the reminder of Tyler and what life was like back then…it's an ebb and flow of past and present. We're better now. So long as we're together. I won't let anything change that.

Reaching up onto the table, Addison's grasp is small and comforting when she lays her hand on my wrist. It's a shock to my system to feel her touch in this moment.

"You okay?" Her question is soft and murmured so no one else can hear.

"Fine," I answer her because it's automatic. I don't tell her more because she doesn't ask. She doesn't let go like I expect her to though. She eats with her left hand, leaving her right on mine. And I leave my hand just where it is, needing to feel that warmth, needing to feel her to make all this regret go away.

So long as I have her, it's all okay. I just need to know I still have her.

Addison

.   .   .

HE's SUPPOSED to be the strong one.

The man is supposed to be the rock. That's what the world leads you to believe, but I think it's bullshit. Why else would I feel more complete, more grounded when I'm trying to hold Daniel together?

Aria and Chloe put a Band-Aid over my pain. They make me forget temporarily, and that's worth something. They make me feel like it's normal to be down right now, and that's worth even more.

But holding on to Daniel, holding him together, that feels like purpose. It feels like belonging and worthiness. One small touch, and it's like the pieces have been soldered back together, making them stronger than they ever were before.

Even if it is just holding his hand and smiling with his family, *my* family.

"Where's Bethany?" Aria asks and my eyes dart to hers although she's slipping her fork into her mouth with her focus on Jase. I know she's asking for my benefit though.

"She couldn't come tonight, but she'll be here tomorrow. She's getting some things adjusted."

"Adjusted?"

"She went through a hard time."

His answer quiets the room for a moment until I speak up. "I'd like to meet her."

Daniel's hand shifts under mine until the back of it is to the table and his palm is against mine.

"I bet you would," Carter comments with the hint of a smile.

"You'll like her," Jase says after a quick drink from his tumbler. The ice clinks as he sets it down on the table. "I don't know anything about what Walsh said, but she may know. If not, you'll still find plenty to talk about."

"Walsh." I roll my eyes as I say his name and take a sip of wine as I feel everyone's eyes on me. The nervousness in the room creeps up a notch. The dark red is sweet, with a hint of lingering decadence. I bring my gaze to Carter's at the head of the table and tell him simply, "He doesn't like me much, I don't think."

"He doesn't like me much either." Jase's response comes with a huff of a laugh from Sebastian as he sits back into his chair with ease, resting an arm over Chloe's chair behind her shoulders.

"He has poor taste then," I offer Jase and that gets me a small laugh from Chloe and her husband. Daniel only observes and half of all my senses are focused on him, focused on me. Everyone's waiting to see if I'm going to break down again. I can feel it. They're waiting to see if I'm okay. And I'm not, I know I'm not. But isn't it okay if I'm not all right?

It sounds like a paradox, but I think it's more real than anything.

Carter takes a deep breath, then says, "He's not

going anywhere soon, but he'll get on board. Or I'll take care of it." His darkly spoken words are overshadowed by Jase's.

"He will," Jase adds and then tells me he's sorry that I felt uncomfortable yesterday. That it never should have happened. He tells me he'd never let anything happen to me. None of them would.

They say we're family, and I know we are.

There's a pit in my gut though when Aria speaks. "Don't worry, Addie, we're in this together."

"Right," I say and nod in agreement, then thank God when I bring the glass up to finish the small pool of wine in it when she tells me, "Nothing bad can happen if we're in it together."

The glass hides my immediate reaction.

I don't know why she says it when she knows that's not true. Bad things happen regardless. Bad things have already happened.

When I set my glass down, I smile at her instead of saying just that. The words still exist though. I can feel them in the tense air. I think everyone can.

Until Chloe stands up abruptly and remembers the cheesecake. She's sweet enough to bring the rest of the bottle in for me too.

"I can't get tipsy with both of you out of commission," I tell her, not wanting to keep drinking in front of them.

"Please, have a glass for me," Aria requests with a yawn.

"I already did," I remind her. The wine was her idea, and not a bad one.

"Then have another one for me." Chloe's cheerful with her pleading eyes and faux pout as she holds out the bottle.

"Well, how can I say no to that?" I jokingly respond to cut the tension in the room more than anything else.

Another round, a plate of sweets, and the story of how Chloe and Sebastian came to be a couple turns the night around. That and the fact that Daniel pulls me into his embrace. My right side is pressed to his hard, toned body, and his stubble gently scratches my hair as he sets his chin on my head and then kisses my crown.

Maybe it works both ways. Back and forth. The rock thing. That makes it difficult, though, when both people are breaking apart.

DANIEL

Her laugh is addictive. It's my drug. The way her cheeks flush, the way her back arches just slightly and her shoulders shake so gently—it all soothes something inside of me that I don't even know is broken until that sweet sound seeps into the crevices and calms the hurt that follows me every day.

That's how I knew I loved her.

The sad, pretty girl who was always around when we were kids smiled easily enough. It wasn't real though. It was a smile that wanted to be more. She wanted to laugh.

And everything inside of me wanted to hear it. I *needed* to hear it.

Just like I needed to hear it tonight. Everyone else's laugh turns to white noise, just like the clinking of the silverware on empty plates and the dull hum of Aria saying something to Carter. All I can hear is Addison's

36

laugh. All I can watch is how her shoulders curl in, and instinctively, her hand finds my lap.

I'm quick to catch it with my own, to squeeze it gently. When she leans into me, humming a small good night to Chloe as she leaves, I kiss her hair and try to memorize everything about this moment.

It's perfect like this. This is how it should be all the time. She should laugh every day. She should smile and reach out to me while she catches her breath with the soft murmur of happiness lingering on her lips.

Every day.

It's easy to say we're broken. It's easy to feel the pain. To hold on to this though — the moments I feel what's really between us — to let ourselves feel it, that's the easiest thing I can do, and the hardest just the same.

"Night." Carter's voice is accompanied by a tight squeeze of my shoulder as they walk behind us.

Addison makes a move to clean up the dishes but Jase reaches for them first, clearing the table and collecting the few remaining dishes in one stack balanced in his left hand. "I got this," he says with a smirk and winks at her. "You cook, we clean."

"Thanks," she tells him and he tells us good night, exiting the room, leaving us to head to bed.

The sound of an empty room is the worst sound. I've spent too much of my life in quiet spaces.

"You had a good time tonight." I hold Addison's hand as we walk, not wanting to let her go just yet.

There were good moments and bad ones too, but I don't mention the tense ones.

Carter or Jase…whoever it was who thought to have the dinner tonight, was right. We never had dinners growing up, not like this. Not after our mom died and everything happened. I could hardly stand to walk into the eat-in kitchen, let alone sit at the table with hope like I did tonight. "We should do it more often."

"Yeah. It was fun," she tells me as we walk down the quiet hall to our wing. The walls are decorated with her photographs. Moments she thought were worthy of capturing on film. Before we get to the bedroom, she stops, lifting her hand from my grasp to touch the edge of a carved black frame mounted against the walls, which are painted a pale dusty blue.

"This one's my favorite of the ones I took while we were away," she says softly.

Her fingertips trace over the glass and down the alley that led to the bar where she first saw me again after so many years had passed.

While we were away. Is that the way she thinks of it?

"I think I like the others better."

"What others?" she says and turns to me quickly, her hair swirling from her shoulder to tumble down her back. Her genuine curiosity makes her eyes widen slightly and it forces my lips to curve up.

"The ones of you in my bed," I answer her and then quickly nip her lower lip as lust just barely reaches her eyes. My blood simmers with desire for her and the need to touch her always.

"You're bad, Daniel Cross," she whispers playfully with passion in her voice as I open the door behind her while letting my lips caress the crook of her neck.

Her eyes are still closed when I pull back. She swallows with a gentle hum and lets her head fall back to rest against the molding that lines the bedroom door.

I find myself trapped in her words. *You're bad, Daniel Cross.*

She knew it all along. She can live with that. She can love me still, even knowing all the wretched things I've done. It's this world though, the world she fled and the world I dragged her back to, that's doing the harm.

I want so badly to blame it on that when I brush the loose strands of her hair off her collarbone with the backs of my fingers so I can kiss her there. I wish I could blame it all on this place. It's only when I stop touching her that she opens her eyes.

A hint of a smile plays at her lips when she finally looks back at me.

"Come to bed with me." I give her the command when we get into the bedroom. With the curtains parted, there's no need to turn on the light. It's dimly lit, but enough so that I can see her perfectly when my eyes adjust. I can see her standing in the doorway, slow to follow me and hesitant to do what I told her.

Hesitant to come to bed with me.

All she's thinking about is the sex. It's not because

she's uncertain if it's safe; the doctor said it was last week. Our first time getting pregnant was an accident. She's questioning if we should try for a baby on purpose.

Whether or not we should try again. Whether we should use protection.

Whether she wants this like I do.

Whether she wants me still… I know that's a question that drifts into her mind when she looks at me like that.

That part of me that doesn't know it's broken until she heals me… it's screaming in pain right now.

"I think I just need to sleep. There's so much on my mind." Her excuse falters in the air as she heads to the dresser, taking off her earrings. I can hear them clink in the small ceramic trinket bowl.

"Tell me," I insist and then clear my throat, pretending like I haven't been devastated every night she's looked at me like that and made some kind of excuse. "Tell me what's on your mind."

"I haven't processed everything."

"You can talk it out with me." I ignore the thump in my chest as I speak. The battering of something hard against my rib cage aches with every small movement.

"Like you talk things out with me?" She turns from the dresser, tense and on the angry side. She seems to realize her quick temper before I can react, crossing her arms over her chest. "Sorry," she apologizes in a hushed murmur. When did it get to be like this? Where we can't talk. The start of a conversation turns into a fight, even if we know we need each other.

Tucking her hair behind her ear, she looks me in the eyes and says, "I know you would... if..."

I close the distance between us and make my way over to finish the thought for her and say, "If that's what you wanted."

"Right," she breathes, the tension leaving her, her arms falling to her side the moment I place my hand on her hip. "It's my fault," she tells me with a harsh swallow.

"Come here," I tell her and my words come out low and rough. There's an edge that's demanding, I know there is. It's a part of me that I'm trying to soften for her. It's still a part of me though.

Falling into my chest and pressing her body as close to mine as she can, she breathes so softly I almost don't hear the admission just under my chin, "I don't know what I want anymore." I tighten my hold on her, wishing I could go back to moments ago. When she was laughing and reaching for me. She confesses, "I'm scared."

It's the first time she's shown me this raw sincerity since we lost the baby.

"It's all right to be scared." With my arm wrapped around her lower back, I splay my hand against her shoulder and rock her slightly, just slightly. She pulls back a tiny bit, only to see me, her chest to mine. I watch as the moonlight filters in from the subtle movement of the curtains, reflecting in her gaze. There's so much vulnerability there. Even now. Even after all we've been through. How much more can she take?

"Kiss me." I give her the command and her posture relaxes, her composure softening the instant her eyes close, and she stands on her tiptoes to bring her lips closer to mine. I keep my eyes open. I watch as she reaches up with both hands, twining her fingers behind my neck as she pushes her lips against mine. She doesn't hesitate this time.

"I love you," she whispers against my lips, peeking up at me through her thick lashes. The curtains sway and bring with them a sudden gust of late-night air, carrying the faint smells of early spring with them.

"I love you too," I tell her, but it's not enough. They're only words that don't compare to what I feel inside.

I'm sorry I put her through all of this. I don't admit it though, because more than sorry, I'm selfish and I wouldn't change it. That's the most fucked-up part. I can't live without her. Even knowing how it breaks her.

"Get ready for bed," she tells me with a weak smile. The smile that's not a smile. The fake one she's always had.

I'm still fully clothed, shoes and all.

The wooden floor creaks in time with her deep inhale as she turns from me and I do as she wishes, letting her take the lead although I don't know how long she'll want it.

"Tell me something and I will," I barter with her.

"I feel lonely," she tells me with her back to me and I can only watch as she pulls the sheets back, sitting on the edge of the bed.

Lonely. Lonely like the quiet halls I hate. Even though I'm right here, it's still lonely. I know she's right.

"Lonely?" I repeat as I drop my watch to the dresser, letting it fall where it may with my gaze still pinned on Addison as she strips down slowly, leaving a puddle of clothes at the side of the bed. She does it every night. She has for the longest time. In the morning, she'll gather them and drop them in the basket. When she has energy; that's the excuse she gave me when I teased her about it before. The memory kicks my lips up into a small smirk, but it fades when I catch her profile in the dark room, the pale light showing me the lack of playfulness, the lack of happiness she's always held on to.

The months we've been back here have worn her down.

"There are moments when I'm okay but they're so fleeting. Recently," she adds quickly. "It's been a lot to take in."

"You don't like being back here, do you?" I question her and that gets her attention.

Turning to face me fully, she doesn't even bother to grab the sheets to cover herself as she answers me with shock clear in her cadence. "Of course I do." She swallows before adding, "I love your family. I've always loved them."

"Things are different now."

"We're all different," she comments without sparing a second between my statement and hers. Her gaze is bold, challenging even. "Just because things are different doesn't mean the pieces I love aren't the same."

I take my time pulling my undershirt over my head and dropping it to the dark wood floor. I strip down to nothing but my boxer briefs before climbing into bed. All the while she watches and waits.

Taking her hand in both of mine, the hand that still doesn't have a ring on it, I run my thumb across its barren finger and ask her, "Did you feel lonely before we lost the baby?"

"No," she answers me quickly and with a slight shake of her head. "It was after. Even with everyone around us… even with you, I just feel lonely sometimes. Like glimpses of loneliness. And I don't know what to do to shake it."

"You aren't alone, and this will pass."

"I know," she admits. "I know. It will pass, but I just don't know what to do in between. I don't know if I'm able to handle it all."

"Do you still want to marry me? You still want to stay here with me?"

"Yes," she answers quickly although she's just as

hasty to look down at our hands. Like she spoke without thinking. Like there's a but.

"Then why no ring?" I ask her quietly and then clear my throat. "Why don't you want to wear it? I asked you to marry me weeks ago. You picked out the ring, but you don't wear it."

"Are you going to wear a ring?" she rebuts.

"An engagement ring?" She nods at the clarification. "Is that what you want? For me to wear a ring?"

Looking past me and out of the cracked window still bringing a gentle breeze, she admits, "No."

"You have to help me understand, Addison." The frustration in my voice is clear as I run a hand down my face and reposition on the bed as I pull my hands away. "It feels like…you aren't completely here with me anymore." Admitting the words makes my chest feel tighter, makes my hands feel colder and numb.

"I'm trying to be," she admits with a single harsh swallow.

"I get wanting to wait to try again," I say, and she tries to interrupt me but I stop her with a finger over her soft lips. "I understand that. It hurts, but I get it. I get that you feel lonely, because I do too. That's what happens when you lose someone. And we did. But I don't understand not wearing my ring. I can wait for you to come back to me and deal with this together; I just need to know that you will or what to do to help you. Losing the baby… I know it's because of everything else. I know it has to do with being here and that you don't love it."

"I never said that."

"You didn't have to."

"I just don't know my place."

"It's next to me. That's your place, with me." My words are rushed and full of frustration.

She starts to speak again, but she has to close her eyes and swallow thickly first, reaching out to me. A moment passes with an uncomfortable pang in my chest. The soft tips of her fingers run down my rough knuckles, tracing scars before she kisses them.

"I want you to wear the ring I got you." She nods once but she still doesn't speak, and she doesn't take her gaze off my knuckles. "I know it's harder, being around my family when the last time you saw them you weren't with me." My words make her still. Every piece of her is frozen as I speak the truth she doesn't say out loud. That's why she's not wearing the ring. It has to be because of that. We came back to the place where she didn't belong to me.

"You're mine now. You're going to find your place and I'll figure out how to help you. We're going to get married. We're going to have a baby one day."

The mention of a baby breaks her composure and I hold her tighter when her face crumples. Kissing her hair, I breathe the words, "I love you and you love me; there's no reason the world shouldn't know that. There's nothing to hide."

"It's not about hiding, it's…it's just everything is…" She trails off as she struggles to voice another word and attempts to move away from me, but I put my hand over hers.

"Just tell me," I say.

"It's never going to just be us. Our past…even right now. It's more than just us and I am struggling."

"Because of Tyler—"

She cuts me off before I can say more. "No. Your other brothers. Your life. *This* life." Breathing in deeper, heavier, she focuses on keeping her breathing steady as she looks me in the eyes to state, "You come with a lot of baggage, Daniel Cross. Some of it, I carry too."

"If this isn't what you want, you shouldn't have come back." I can't describe the way my blood chills and everything hardens. My jaw, my stiff back, the thump in my chest that quiets to a dull ache.

"I know, it's all my fault." The hurt in her voice reflects in her gaze.

"Stop saying that. We're in this together. None of this is your fault."

She looks like she'll say something, but all she does is nod slightly, refusing to open up and tell me what's going on in that beautiful head of hers.

"Don't keep it from me."

"I'm struggling to handle it; I need help."

"Tell me how."

"I just can't wear your ring," she confesses weakly.

"What part of not wearing my ring is supposed to help you?"

"Are you so dense, Daniel?" The contempt is unexpected. "You gave it to me after I found out. You gave me a ring because I was pregnant. That's the only reason. And we never should have gotten pregnant. It was an accident. I wasn't ready. It's my fault!"

"Addison—"

"I'm doing my best and I'm highly aware that it's not good enough. I couldn't even carry our baby," she says, and the last two words are a strangled mess between the shuddering sob she holds back.

"Don't say that… You are more than enough." I stress my words, grasping both of her hands in mine firmly and holding her gaze with mine to steady her. "Not a damn thing is your fault. Nothing but keeping all of this from me and letting it tear us apart. You have to talk to me."

"You have to talk to me too." She whimpers the plea as her watery eyes look up to mine.

"I can do that." I'm quick to acquiesce to her request. "I can talk to you, but you have to tell me if it's too much."

"It's all too much," she admits, "but I still want it. I still want you."

The relief that blooms inside of me is instant. It's everything I needed.

"One thing at a time." I wait for her to nod at my words, to know she's listening. "You are more than good enough. You're too good for me, but I'm keeping you anyway."

"Daniel—"

"No." I don't let her interrupt me. "You got to tell me, now it's my turn to tell you."

"Okay," she whispers, her grip getting tighter as she waits.

"You are with me and I am with you. We can't let each other be lonely. I'm right here," I whisper against the shell of her ear and then plant a gentle kiss against the tender skin beneath her ear. "We're going to be okay. You're going to find your place…so long as it's right next to me. We have to talk. We can't hold it in." I'm careful with my next suggestion. "You don't know your place, because you don't know what's going on. I want to tell you. I want you to know."

"The stress…" The words leave her sounding more like a helpless question than a statement.

"I think it will help, not hurt to know. It's the not knowing that's stressful."

She doesn't respond even though I give her time to.

"Do you think you'd be all right with that? Instead of you asking, I just tell and if it's too much, you tell me to stop and I will."

"Will that help you?" she questions me. The hope in her voice is there, but it's surprising that it comes with this particular question.

I almost tell her I'm fine. I'm so close to saying just that. Which would defeat the purpose of all of this.

"Yes. It fucking kills me that I can't tell you what's eating at me."

"Okay then. New rules. You tell me everything unless I say stop." Fear and hope swirl in her glossy gaze.

"The loss is something we have to go through together and maybe we'll have moments where we feel alone, because we were wishing those moments were with the little life we never got to hold. But if you can try to remember I'm here, I hope it will help."

She swallows her words rather than responding. I keep going though. I'll take the lead and she'll follow. She has to. I don't know how this can work otherwise.

"I gave you the ring because I love you. The only reason I didn't give it to you sooner was because I wasn't sure you'd say yes. I thought I had a little anchor knowing you were pregnant. It wasn't an obligation because you were pregnant. It wasn't that, Addison. Don't think that."

She searches my expression, maybe in an attempt to determine if I'm sincere or not. It's what I deserve. Years ago, I kept everything from her, for a very long time. Our relationship started with lies, and it's carried on with secrets. She'll learn to trust me though. She has to. I won't give her any reason not to.

"I want you to wear my ring. I want you to come to bed with me, be with me again, even if you want to be safe and wait to try again. I need you, Addison."

It feels like I've emptied everything out. Leaving me

hollow and waiting with nothing but the hope that she'll know this is all I've got. It's everything, every bit of me, and I don't know if it's enough but I'm damn sure going to try.

"I need you too," she finally whispers in the warm air between us, making it feel even hotter than it already is. I'm still on edge, waiting and needing more of her.

"Tell me we're going to be all right. That you're going to be all right." It's a command.

"I'm going to try," she answers, and I know it's because she wants to be honest and that she doesn't actually believe it. She doesn't know deep in her bones that it'll work. It never has before.

"You're going to succeed. You are meant to be with me, Addison. There's no way this ends otherwise. I need you and I need my family." I suck in a breath, ready to tell her if we have to, we'll leave. We did it before; we can do it again. It'll kill me, but for her, I'd do it.

"I need them too," she says, quick to cut me off. "I want this to work. Not just us; we work, and I love you, but this place. I just...I don't know."

"You don't know, that's exactly it. You don't know anything and that's the problem. I'll fix it. We'll fix this."

"I don't know that I can handle it," she confesses with a quivering bottom lip. "I've never felt so insignificant and weak." As she speaks, her voice goes dry and cracks at the words.

"I've put you through hell, and you survived."

"They've gone through worse. Aria—"

"Don't compare your story to hers; it doesn't change your pain." She's unraveling in front of me. Six months of being here and I've never seen her like this. How did I let it get this bad? "Get on the bed. In the center."

"Daniel—"

"The bed. Get in the middle, now." I emphasize my words and slowly pull away from her, keeping my gaze pinned to hers. "You can handle it, Addison. You can take everything."

Her shoulders drop heavily as she swallows, and her chest rises faster with every breath as she stares back at me. Not moving.

"I need you, Addison, and you need me. That's why we're off, why everything feels wrong. Get on the bed."

I've never had to repeat myself. She's always listened before, and staring at her now, not knowing what she'll do, I can't breathe. I can't lose her.

"On the bed, Addison. Don't make me tell you again."

* * *

Addison

I'VE LOVED this man since before I knew what love was.

I've craved him, adored him, fucking worshipped him.

But never like this. An intense heat ignites inside of me, a spark hotter and brighter than the sun dances on every nerve ending in my body.

I'm paralyzed, needing to feel him take me, own me, and devour me exactly how he wants.

I need it more than he'll ever know.

Slowly, I obey, although I don't know how. Every movement is gentle and meticulous. My hands reach the center first and immediately my fingers dig into the mattress.

It's so slow. Time moves so slowly. A part of me knows it's because I'm trying to remember this moment. Remember it all and hold on to it forever. I need it in the good times and the bad. In the horrible moments, I need this. What we have right now. I wish I could just stay here forever. Being his and him being so completely mine.

Bared to him, I wait and watch. His cock is hard and ready as he strokes himself in front of me, pacing, debating what he wants me to do, what he needs from me.

All the while, those sparks tingle up and down my body in waves of want.

Instead of climbing on the bed, pinning me down, and ravaging me, he asks me, "Why do I love you?"

His words are hoarse and at first I hear him wrong.

I hear, "Why do you love me?" but I catch myself before the answer can leave me.

"I don't know," I answer him.

Instead of answering me, he tells me to spread my legs wide so he can see me.

"Fuck, I can see how wet you are from here," he breathes out deep with frustration as my fingertips run along the length of my pussy and then rub my swollen clit so he can see. A shiver of desire runs down my body from my shoulders to the tips of my toes. It's cold compared to the heat that burns between my thighs for him to enter me.

"Why do I love you?"

I close my eyes, pushing my head back into the mattress, and move my hand away, hating that I don't know what to tell him.

I don't know why people fall in love. I know why I love him though; I want to answer him that. *Ask me something I know.*

"Eyes on me. Don't you dare close your eyes." His steps are hard as he rounds the bed, getting close enough to backhand the inside of my thigh as punishment. The sting is fierce, but the touch is so needed, all I feel is a spike of desire shoot through me.

My breath is stolen from his admonishment, seething through my teeth and desperate.

"Put your fingers back on that pretty cunt of yours and look me in the eyes when you tell me you don't know why I love you." There's no hurt in his eyes, no pain in his voice, even though I feel it, deep down inside of me. Past everything physical, I feel it.

Tears prick at the back of my eyes as I let my fingers touch my warmth. His gaze parts from mine, only to watch me.

I have to give him something, so I tell him what I know. I tell him why I love him, praying he loves me the same.

"You know I've wanted you for as long as we've known each other. You know I'd risk it all to be with you."

My fingers slip just inside my entrance as I start to say the next reason, and a soft moan spills from my lips in its place.

"Fuck," he mutters. The word is a groan on Daniel's lips and hearing it makes my body heat.

"Touch me please," I beg him, but he shakes his head.

"Why else?" he asks huskily, the need showing through his intended words.

"You know that I would die without you. Whatever makes a person a person—I'd die if you weren't here anymore."

"I don't want you to ever say that again. Don't you ever talk about that. You're not allowed to die."

A short laugh that's not humorous at all bubbles from my lips. I feel crazy, on the verge of tears, feeling the pain of a great loss at the very thought that he might die. "That's my fear. It kills me, Daniel. You can't die."

"Well, for you then, I'll do my best not to," he tells me as the bed dips with his weight while he climbs over my body.

Pinning my wrists above my head, he nearly kisses my lips, but he moves to suck the arousal off my fingertips before our lips touch. The light, warm feeling is a stark contrast to his hard cock pressed into my thigh.

I try to writhe under him, but he keeps me still as he takes his time. The second he braces his forearm beside my head and positions himself, I suck in a deep breath and stare into his dark eyes.

He enters me slowly, torturously so. Taking his time to stretch me. The gentle sting elicits an instant heated wave that forces my back to arch. He doesn't stop, he just pushes in deeper and stays there, pressing against my walls and forcing my lips to form a perfect O.

Still inside of me, he tells me, "Because I want to grow old with you. I want everything you want, whatever it is, because it'll make you happy. I want my family to love you and protect you, in case something ever happens to me.

"You don't want those things unless you love that person. I love you more than I love myself, Addison. I need you to know that."

I only know I'm crying because he bends down to kiss the tears.

When his lips finally brush against mine, I steal them, kissing him hard and with the passion I have for him, for what's between us.

With his left hand still pinning my wrists down, he ravages me, a savage taking of what's his. I scream my pleasure into his mouth, letting the strangled moans take over when my climax hits me with a force I've never felt before.

It's all consuming. It's everything I've wanted and needed and the only thing I'll ever crave for as long as I live. Because it's him.

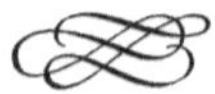

"It's a pretty ring." The timid voice carries across the large kitchen. "Blue under it; that's unique. Is it a blue diamond?"

I didn't even hear her walk in. As I stirred the sugar into my coffee, watching the white swirl of steam, I was focused on the ache between my thighs and the memory of Daniel kissing me all over last night.

He only left me to get the ring from my nightstand and to put it on my finger. If this ring ever comes off my hand, it'll be because someone took it from my grave.

"It is. It reminds me of forget-me-nots," I answer her. "That's why we went with this one."

"You picked out your ring together?"

"I know it's not traditional—"

"What is anymore?" she says and shrugs. "If you

haven't guessed, I'm Bethany." The smile she gives me reaches her eyes.

I laugh, short and with a single breath. It's genuine. "I guessed as much," I answer her with a smile.

It's only us in the kitchen and as she pulls out one of the tall chairs at the island, the sound carries through the open space.

"First, I want to say hi. Second, I want to say I'm sorry. Jase told me…about the baby."

My little piece of heaven splinters, but only slightly as I take my seat.

"Thank you," I answer her.

Holding on to my mug of coffee, I pull it up to my lips to keep me from saying more. The warmth billows into my face as I take a long sip, praying for composure.

I don't want to break down. Especially not in front of her, someone I don't know. This…Bethany Fawn. I don't know that I'll ever be okay with losing our baby. Especially if we never get pregnant again, if we never have a little one to hold. I don't see how it's possible. I don't think there's anything wrong with that either.

"I heard you got a ring too," I say as I lift a brow and when her gaze catches mine, I make a note of staring down at her ring finger. She pulls her hand into her chest with a blush rising to her cheeks.

"It was a shock, to be honest," she answers but the content note in her voice and the smile on her face remain the same. "We're quite different…Jase and I," she adds when I look questioningly at her.

"Yes, they are…different. That's a word for it." We could write a book about the Cross brothers and how *different* they are. There's a time and place for that conversation though. "So Jase told me your last name is Fawn?"

"It is."

"Mother or father?" I ask her and then shake my head as I let out a sigh at my ridiculousness. "This isn't an inquisition. I'm just… I'm very curious."

"It's fine," she responds and then she leans forward on the chair to rest on the counter. Her thin cream sweater is pushed up to her elbows. Paired with her dark blue jeans, it's a simple look, but something about this woman screams that she's anything but simple.

"My father's last name, but he didn't stick around after I was born."

"My father's last name as well," I tell her and feel a chill sweep over my skin.

"You're a couple years younger than me, right?" she questions me and I nod. Daniel told me what he knew of Bethany.

"A little over a year younger."

"What's your father's first name?" I ask her as my gaze sweeps over her facial features. She doesn't look like me, nothing but her lips. My father's lips.

"Jeremy," she answers, and I tell her the middle name, "Nathanial. Jeremy Nathanial Fawn."

"This is weird." Bethany pushes out the same thought I have.

"I think your dad left your mom because my mom was pregnant with me." The years make sense. "That's why you didn't grow up with him." Not that I grew up with him either. He left my mother and my mother left me.

"So he knocked up my mom and had my sister. Married her and they had me. Then he left us when I was a baby, because your mother was pregnant with you?" Bethany fills in the blanks.

"He got around, as if I needed another reason to hate the thought of him."

"My mother had substance abuse issues; I always thought that was why he left us," Bethany muses. "He was good at leaving," she comments with a crease in her forehead, as though a bad memory is creating a groove right there. "That's what my mother used to say." She doesn't try to hide the bitterness as she turns her back to me, leaving her seat so she can go to a cabinet to get herself a mug. I note that she already knows where they're kept and where everything else in the room is too.

"If it makes you feel any better, he didn't stay long and what I knew of my mother and the men she was with, it's probably best you grew up without him." With another sip of coffee, the room's quiet except for the muffled hiss of the coffee machine. I don't comment that I was a child when I knew them. Either of them.

"Yet we both received his last name," Bethany says as she leans against the cabinet and then offers me a half smile curved with sarcasm before lifting her mug and telling me cheers. "Lucky us."

"If we hadn't, we never would have known."

"We're sisters. Same father, different mother."

"Right." I nod in understanding. Curiosity nags at the back of my mind, but I can't bring myself to ask her any questions. That part of my life is long behind me. I wish it would stay in the past. I don't want to think about my father or how many other children he had.

"Do you have any other siblings?" she asks me and I shake my head no as I reply, "All I had growing up was a rotating address until I met…" I pause and wave my hand in the air. My throat's dry but I shake it off. I'm stronger because of what I went through. But that doesn't mean I want to relive it with this woman. Biological sister or not. My curiosity can wait until I'm better prepared and in a more stable state. Everything is chaos now and it doesn't look like she's going anywhere anyway.

"The Cross brothers," she answers for me. "So you knew them before all this? Back when things weren't so…"

"Yeah, but I left. I left before a lot of things happened. I left when things got bad. What a wonderful mother I'll be." All of our past history hits me at once and the same thoughts I had before, the ones that tell me I don't deserve Daniel, I don't deserve a happily ever after, and I don't deserve to be a mother come back. Weaker than before, they're only whispers and not screams. Nonetheless, they're back.

"Don't say that. You were young and you didn't know. You'll be a great mother. I hardly know you, but I know that. We'll be better than our parents."

"How can you know?"

"One, because you're already thinking about it. Already wanting more for your children. And two, because we're loved. Love does… Love changes a person.

"The best thing you can do for a child is to love them. You can ask anyone that. It's the thing they need most. If you love Daniel and he loves you, you're already off to a better start than our parents."

"God knows one thing these men do is love hard," I comment, agreeing with her and hoping she's right. "Even with all the shit they're in."

"They do," she agrees with me, casually reaching in the fridge for creamer. As if this is only a mundane conversation and not the turning point in my life that I feel it is in my bones.

"So you're going to try again?" she asks me.

I want to tell her I'm scared. Scared to try, scared to lose. Scared I won't be good enough. But I save those sentiments for Daniel. If I tell anyone, it should be him.

So I answer simply, "Yes." I want a baby with him. A

life. I want to grow old with him and be surrounded by a loving family. To love and be loved. "We're going to try again."

"I just need to know." A raw hint of emotion makes Carter's voice tight. He clears his throat as he leans back in the chair. "I would understand; I just need to be prepared and we can work something out." His voice is clearer, firmer, but he still can't look me in the eyes.

"I'm not leaving. There's nothing else for me. I can't leave."

"But Addison—" he argues, already having it in his head that we need to leave.

"She doesn't want to leave either." It's quiet for a moment, then Carter finally looks at me, letting the statement sink in. "We're staying and we'll be all right."

The ticking of the clock in his office is ever present. It fills the silence until he nods in agreement.

"A lot happened," he comments.

"It will settle down. It'll slow down."

A knock at the office door accompanies his hum of agreement.

"It will," he tells me before calling out, "Come in" to whoever it is at the door.

Addison.

"Am I interrupting?" Her question is softly spoken, but it carries through the room clearly as she stands there, not in the room, but not out of it either.

"Not at all," Carter answers. His shoulders are straighter, his expression firmer. He really thought we were going to leave. He has the look of a man who'd already accepted loss.

"I was hoping to talk to both of you…" She trails off as her gaze drops to the floor nervously before peeking back up at us. "I had a thought."

A prick of uncertainty creeps along my spine as she slowly walks into the room and stops at the chair next to mine. With her grip on the back of it, she chooses not to sit as she tells us, "I want to pay a visit to Officer Walsh."

"The hell you are." My answer is immediate. And also ignored. Addison's stare is unmoving and directed at Carter.

He doesn't answer, neither of them looking at me.

"The fuck you are," I say to emphasize my position. "There's no reason for you to be anywhere near him."

"Other than the fact that I'm with you. That my place is beside you…so yeah, there is."

Carter's still quiet and the ticking of the clock is louder, just like the rush of my blood is in my ears.

"Daniel," she says, and Addison's tone is gentle.

"No. You shouldn't be concerned with this."

"I don't want to be mixed up in this, but I don't want to be afraid of this man. I don't want him to think he can get to me."

"Are you sure you want to do that? You getting involved is more…" Carter talks to her, again, ignoring me.

The irritation grows as the two of them discuss this as though it's a casual conversation.

"Stress? No. I think the stress comes from not knowing. I need to know. And if I can do something, I need to do it."

"I don't want you to—"

"To go to a police station? Where you have plenty of men in your back pocket?" Addison cuts me off and slight desperation seeps into her cadence. "I…" She pauses and swallows thickly. "I want you to think about it. Think about what I should be doing and what it would do for me." She puts her hand over mine to tell me, "I want to do this. I want to show that man who I am and that I'm with you. With all of you," she amends, giving Carter a nod.

"Just think about it." She leaves me there, my foot subconsciously tapping against the leg of the chair. The second the office door closes, I admonish my brother,

"You couldn't back me up with that one?" The sarcasm is thick and unforgiving.

"You weren't lying, were you? She does want to stay."

For the first time in a long time, my brother smiles.

"If she wants to stay, then, Daniel, for the love of God, let her. Let her do what she needs to do."

"Two sets of eyes are on his office in case he shuts the door."

"I know," I answer Daniel.

"If we lose sight for even a moment, I'm coming in."

"I know," I repeat and even though I'm attempting to sound agitated, I'm anything but. "You're cute when you're worried."

His short huff is humorless, coming deep from his chest as we sit in the car.

"In and out, Addison," he tells me, leaning over the console to give me a peck on the cheek. I don't kiss him back, because I'm waiting, and sure enough, he asks again.

"You sure you want to do this?"

The way he asks it melts everything inside of me. I don't answer him with words; instead I put a hand on either side of his handsome face, feeling his stubble beneath my palms, and press a gentle kiss to his lips. His dark eyes are open and staring down at me when I pull away.

"I'll be right back," I murmur.

"And I'll be right here."

As I shut the door to the car, I hear him say he's starting the clock. I have five minutes. That's what he gave me and I'm just fine with that.

If I'm going to be here with Daniel, as his wife and as a part of his family, I'm going to make sure everyone knows exactly where I stand.

Even with that confidence, my heart hammers as I walk through the dark glass doors to the station. Officer Walsh's office is upstairs on the second floor. The elevator is empty, which doesn't ease my nerves at all. I have to shake out my clammy hands and give myself a pep talk.

I'm merely planning to apologize for being caught off guard. To thank Officer Walsh for asking if I was all right and to let him know that I'm more than all right and not to question where I stand with the Cross brothers again.

Daniel and his brothers told me where Walsh's office is. It's the back-right corner office. I'm glad I know where it is and that when I finally get close, his door is open and he's right in view. Alone, unsuspecting. Just like I was when he approached me.

It's hard to give him the benefit of the doubt. That

he's only a cop looking out for a woman who's mixed up with men like the Cross brothers.

I try to keep it in mind as I raise my fist to the open door and knock gently.

Words were nearly spoken as he lifts his head, but when Cody Walsh sees me, they're silenced and instead he's slow to tap the papers in his hands on the desk. "Miss Fawn."

"Officer Walsh." I speak his name pleasantly. Forgetting the pounding of adrenaline in my blood and noting that he's only a man. Nothing more than human.

"I thought I'd see you again," he comments. "Please come in."

It's quiet for a moment as I try to get ahold of my bearings.

He speaks first, easing the tension. "You'll have to forgive my first impression. I don't know what to make of the relationships they have. Your fiancé and his brothers."

"Relationships?" I question, raising a brow and deciding to make light of it. "If Daniel has more than one of me…well, no wonder he's so stressed."

The short chuckle eases the officer slightly as he leans back in his chair, but his guard is still up. Something tells me it always is.

"Have a seat," he offers, and I shake my head, telling him I was just stopping by for a quick moment.

"I'm not the bad guy, you know?" he tells me, catching me off guard.

"I didn't say you were."

"You didn't have to," he responds solemnly. "I'm still getting a read on them and you didn't seem like you were all right," he explains although he doesn't have to.

"He's not a bad guy either." And I defend Daniel, although I don't have to.

"I didn't say he was."

It's quiet for a moment and I debate saying what's on my mind. I nearly don't but I decide I may never have another chance, so I should take it.

"You shouldn't have mentioned my past. The foster…situation. Without it, you would have seemed like less of a bad guy."

"Without it, I wouldn't have known whether or not you knew."

I hum in agreement, nodding although I don't take my eyes off of his.

"What do I owe this visit to?" he asks when I go quiet, taking him in and trying to see where he falls. It changes with every passing minute. "Did you have a message for me?" he questions.

"As if I'd do their dirty work? No, I don't have a message. I'm not privy to those conversations, Mr. Walsh. As you know, I appear to be the last to know most things around here." Lying comes easier than I thought it would. In fact, I kind of like it. There's a devilish spark that riddles its way through me as he asks me, "And you're okay with that?"

I'm not okay with it. But that's one thing that's changing. Daniel's right. I need to know. I was always meant to be a part of this. I *need* this.

Reaching into my purse, I pull out a Tupperware of fresh-baked cookies.

"For you," I say while offering the small container. "I made a larger batch, but not all of them survived."

He rises out of his seat but stops short of taking them for only a moment before accepting the gift. "Snickerdoodles?"

I shrug and say, "Cinnamon makes people happy."

"You made me cookies?"

"I was having a bad day; I was short with you and I apologize."

"I apologize as well; I sometimes forget that not every conversation is an interrogation."

Looking at the clock on the wall above his head, I see five minutes has already passed. Half of me is surprised Daniel isn't here, waiting behind me. The other half is relieved he's given me this. I can handle this, and I want him to know it.

Patting the lid of the Tupperware, I offer him a smile and say, "I hope you like them. And I hope you know where I stand now."

· · ·

His statement keeps me from turning and leaving like I'd planned. "I'm just wondering what you see in him." Officer Walsh doesn't look at me with curiosity; it's simply matter-of-fact. "From what I read, you had a hard upbringing, you fell into step with a group of brothers who took care of your problems, but then you took off. You'd gotten away, you made a new life, and then you came back... Why? Why come back to this?"

"To them, you mean." It's not a question that comes from me so easily, it's a correction. "You obviously don't know them well...yet," I add. "If you knew them, you'd know why."

His chair groans as he heaves back. It gives with the pressure of his back pushing against it and then he clicks his tongue. He seems to debate his words and then he jokes, of all things, lightening the tension, "It's because he's good-looking, isn't it?"

I let a small laugh leave me before I playfully respond, "He's handsome. He has a really charming smile...but you should hear him laugh."

My heart does a funny thing at the memory of it from just the other night.

The officer's rough chuckle doesn't compare in the least. He's a handsome man, on the right side of the law, with power and a strength that any woman would find attractive. But he's not my damaged hero. He's not a part of my family.

He's a pawn in their game and I'm content in doing my part.

"Are you sure you know what you're doing?" he asks me just as I turn my back to him, and my smile nearly falters. Nearly, but I hold it in place.

Turning back around and leaning forward, I have to lower my voice and whisper as though what I'm telling him is a secret. "I'm absolutely certain."

I leave without another word, but before the door closes to his office, I hear him say, "I really hope you are."

The ghost of a smile on my lips doesn't leave; it stays right where it is even though I feel a chill down my spine. It grows colder with every step. Among the clatter of keyboards, phones ringing, and the white noise of the officers and secretaries talking, I hear the click of heels clearly. They're in time with the beat of my heart.

It's not until I'm outside of the double-doored station and a gust of wind blows my hair over my shoulders, tickling up my neck, that the chill leaves me. With a deep breath, I search for the car, finding it quickly, with Daniel leaning against it.

He is my home. He is my person. Beside him is where I belong, and I'll do whatever it takes to stay there. Every sacrifice it demands, I'll make.

Carter's story, Merciless, is available now!
Keep reading for a sneak peek …

. . .

Daniel and Addison's story started with Possessive, click here to start from the very beginning.

* * *

Want a signed copy of Seductive or any of my other books? Shop here and use **ebook20 to save 20%**. Coupon also works on bookish merch in my shop. Happy shopping xoxo

Click here to sign up to my mailing list, where you'll get *exclusive* giveaways, free books and new release alerts!

Follow me on Bookbub to be the first to know about my sales!

Sign up for Text Alerts:
US residents: Text WILLOW to 797979
UK residents: Text WWINTERS to 82228

And if you're on Facebook, join my reader group, Willow Winters' Wildflowers for special updates and lots of fun!

SNEAK PEEK AT MERCILESS

From *USA Today* bestselling author W Winters comes a heart-wrenching, edge-of-your-seat gripping, romantic suspense.

I should've known she would ruin me the moment I saw her.

Women like her are made to destroy men like me.

I couldn't resist her though.

Given to me to start a war; I was too eager to accept.

But I didn't know what she'd do to me. That she would change everything.

She sees through me in a way no one else ever has.

Her innocence and vulnerability make me weak for her and I hate it.

I know better than to give in to temptation.

A ruthless man doesn't let a soul close to him.

A cold-hearted man doesn't risk anything for anyone.

A powerful man with a beautiful woman at his mercy … he doesn't fall for her.

CHAPTER 1

CARTER

War is coming.

It's something I've known for over two years.

Tick. Tock. Tick. Tock.

My jaw ticks in time with the skin over my knuckles turning white as my fist clenches tighter. The tension in my stiff shoulders rises and I have to remind myself to breathe in deep and let the strain of it all go away.

Tick. Tock. It's the only sound echoing off the walls of my office and with each passing of the pendulum the anger grows.

It's always like this before I go to a meet. This one in particular sends a thrill through my blood, the adrenaline pumping harder with each passing minute.

My gaze moves from the grandfather clock in my office to the shelves next to it and then beneath them to the box made of mahogany and steel. It's only three feet deep and tall and six feet long. It blends into the right wall of my office, surrounded by polished bookshelves that carry an aroma of old books.

I paid more than I should have simply to put on display. All any of this is a façade. People's perceptions are their reality. And so I paint the picture they need to see so I can use them as I see fit. The expensive books and paintings, polished furniture made of rare wood… All of it is bullshit.

Except for the box. The story that came with it will stay with me forever. In all of the years, it's the one of the few memories that I can pin point as a defining moment. The box never leaves me.

The words from the man who gave it to me are still as clear as is the memory of his pale green eyes, glassed over as he told me his story.

About how it kept him safe when he was a child. He told me how his mother had shoved him in it to protect him.

I swallow thickly, feeling my throat tighten and the cord in my neck strain with the memory. He painted the picture so well.

He told me how he clung to his mother seeing how panicked she was. But he did as he was told, he stayed quiet in the safe box and could only listen while the men murdered his mother.

It was the story he gave me with the box he offered

to barter for his life. And it reminded me of my own mother telling me goodbye before she passed.

Yes, his story was touching, but the defining moment is when I put the gun to his head and pulled the trigger regardless.

He tried to steal from me and then pay me with a box as if the money he laundered was a debt or a loan. William was good at stealing, at telling stories, but the fucker was a dumb prick.

I didn't get to where I am by playing nicely and being weak. That day I took the box that saved him as a reminder of who I was. Who I needed to be.

I made sure that box has been within my sight for every meeting I've had in this office. It's a reminder for me so I can stare at it in this god forsaken room as I make deal after deal with criminal after criminal and collect wealth and power like the dusty old books on these shelves.

It cost me a fortune to get this office exactly how I wanted. But if it were to burn down, I could buy it all over again.

Everything except for that box.

"You really think they're going through with it?" I hear Daniel, my brother, before I see him. The memories fade in an instant and my heart beat races faster than the tick tock of that fucking clock.

It takes a second for me to be conscious of my facial expression, to relax it and let go of the anger before I can raise my gaze to his.

"With the war and the deal? You think he'll go through with it?" he clarifies.

A small huff leaves me, accompanied by a smirk, "He wants this more than anything else," I answer him.

Daniel stalks into the room slowly, the heavy door to my office closing with a soft kick of his heel before he comes to stand across from me.

"And you're sure you want to be right in the middle of it?"

I lick my lower lip and stand from my desk, stretching as I do and turning my gaze to the window in my office. I can hear Daniel walking around the desk as I lean against it and cross my arms.

"We won't be in the middle of it. It'll be the two of them, our territory is close, but we can stay back."

"Bullshit. He wants you to fight with him and he's going to start this war tonight and you know it."

I nod slowly, the smell of Romano's cigars filling my lungs at the memory of him.

"There's still time to call it off," Daniel says and it makes my brow pinch and place a crease on my forehead. He can't be that naïve.

It's the first time I've really looked at him since he's been back. He spent years away. And every fucking day I fought for what we have. He's gone soft. Or maybe it's Addison that's turned him into the man standing in front of me.

"This war has to happen." My words are final and the tone is one not to be questioned. I may have grown this business on fear and anger. Each step forward followed by the hollow sound of a body dropping behind me, but that's not how it started. Y can't build an empire with blood stained hands and not expect death to follow you.

His dark eyes narrow as he pushes off the desk and moves closer to the window, his gaze flickering between me and the meticulously maintained garden stories below us.

"Are you sure you want to do this?" his voice is low and I barely hear it. He doesn't look back at me and a chill flows down my arms and the back of my neck as I take in his stern expression.

It takes me back years ago. Back to when we had a choice and chose wrong.

When whether or not we wanted to go through with it meant something.

"There are men to the left of us," I tell him as I step forward and close the distance between us. "There are men to the right. There is no possible outcome where we don't pick a side."

He nods once and slides his thumb across the stubble on his chin before looking back at me. "And the girl?" he asks me, his eyes piercing into mine and reminding me that both of us survived, both of us fought, and each of us has a tragic path that led us to where we are today.

"Aria?" I dare to speak her name and the sound of my smooth voice seems to linger in the space between us. I don't wait for him to acknowledge me, or her rather.

"She has no choice." My voice tightens as I say the words.

Clearing my throat, I lean my palms against the window, feeling the frigid fall beneath my hands and leaning forward to see Addison beneath us, Daniel's Addison. "What do you think they would have done to Addison if they'd succeeded in taking her?"

His jaw hardens but he doesn't answer my question. Instead he replies, "We don't know who it was who tried to take her from me."

I shrug as if it's semantics and not at all relevant. "Still. Women aren't meant to be touched, but they went for Addison first."

"That doesn't make it right," Daniel says with indignation in his tone.

"Isn't it better she come to us?" My head tilts as I question him and this time he takes a moment to respond.

"She's not one of us. Not like Addison and you know what Romano expects you to do with her."

"Yes, the daughter of the enemy…" My heart beats hard in my chest, and the steady rhythm reminds me of the ticking of the clock. "I know exactly what he wants me to do with her."

Click here to keep reading Merciless!

They lived on the same street and went to the same school, although he was a year ahead. Even so close, he was untouchable.

Sebastian was bad news and Chloe was the sad girl who didn't belong.

Then one night changed everything.

Possessive (a standalone novel)

It was never love with **Daniel Cross** and she never thought it would be. It was only lust from a distance. Unrequited love maybe.

He's a man Addison could never have, for so many reasons.

Merciless Saga

Merciless

Heartless

Breathless

Endless

Ruthless, crime family leader **Carter Cross** should've known Aria would ruin him the moment he saw her. Given to Carter to start a war; he was too eager to accept. But what he didn't know was what Aria would do to him. He didn't know that she would change everything.

All He'll Ever Be (Merciless Series Collection of all 4 novels)

Irresistible Attraction Trilogy
A Single Glance
A Single Kiss
A Single Touch

Bethany is looking for answers and to find them she needs one of the brothers of an infamous crime family, **Jase Cross**.
Even a sizzling love affair won't stop her from getting what she needs.
But Bethany soon comes to realise Jase will be her downfall, and she's determined to be his just the same.

Irresistible Attraction (A Single Glance Trilogy Collection)

Hard to Love Series
Hard to Love
Desperate to Touch
Tempted to Kiss
Easy to Fall

Eight years ago she ran from him.
Laura should have known he'd come for her. Men like **Seth King** always get what they want.
Laura knows what Seth wants from her, and she knows it comes with a steep price.
However it's a risk both of them will take.

Not My Heart to Break (Hard to Love Series
Collection)

Tease Me Once
I'll Kiss You Twice
Tease me once... I'll kiss you twice.
Declan Cross' story from the Merciless World.

Spin off of the Merciless World

Love the Way Duet
Kiss Me
Hold Me
Love Me

With everything I've been through, and the
unfortunate way we met, the last thing I thought I'd be
focused on is the fact that I love the way you kiss me.

Extended epilogues to the Merciless World Novels
A Kiss To Keep (more of Sebastian and Chloe)
Seductive (more of Daniel and Addison)
Effortless (more of Carter and Aria)
Never to End (more of Seth and Laura)

**Sexy, thrilling with a touch of dark Standalone
Novels**

Broken (Standalone)

Kade is ruthless and cold hearted in the criminal world.
They gave Olivia to him. To break. To do as he'd like.
All because she was in the wrong place at the wrong time. But there are secrets that change everything. And once he has her, he's never letting her go.

Forget Me Not (Standalone novel)
She loved a boy a long time ago. He helped her escape and she left him behind. Regret followed her every day after.
Jay, the boy she used to know, came back, a man. With a grip strong enough to keep her close and a look in his eyes that warned her to never dare leave him again.
It's dark and twisted.
But that doesn't make it any less of what it is.
A love story. Our love story.

<u>It's Our Secret</u> (Standalone novel)
It was only a little lie. That's how stories like these get started.
But with every lie Allison tells, **Dean** sees through it.
She didn't know what would happen. But with all the secrets and lies, she never thought she'd fall for him.

You Are Mine Series of Duets

You Are My Reason (You Are Mine Duet book 1)
You Are My Hope (You Are Mine Duet book 2)

Mason and Jules emotionally gripping romantic suspense duet.
One look and Jules was tempted; one taste, addicted.
No one is perfect, but that's how it felt to be in Mason's arms.
But will the sins of his past tear them apart?

You Know I Love You
You Know I Need You
Kat says goodbye to the one man she ever loved even though **Evan** begs her to trust him.
With secrets she couldn't have possibly imagined, Kat is torn between what's right and what was right for them.

Tell Me You Want Me
A sexy office romance with a brooding hero, **Adrian Bradford**, who you can't help but fall head over heels for... in and out of the boardroom.

Small Town Romance

Tequila Rose Book 1
Autumn Night Whiskey Book 2
He tasted like tequila and the fake name I gave him was Rose.
Four years ago, I decided to get over one man, by getting under another. A single night and nothing more.

Now, with a three-year-old in tow, the man I still dream about is staring at me from across the street in the town I grew up in. I don't miss the flash of recognition, or the heat in his gaze.
The chemistry is still there, even after all these years.
I just hope the secrets and regrets don't destroy our second chance before it's even begun.

A Little Bit Dirty

Contemporary Romance Standalones

Knocking Boots (A Novel)

They were never meant to be together.
Charlie is a bartender with noncommittal tendencies.
Grace is looking for the opposite. Commitment. Marriage. A baby.

Promise Me (A Novel)
She gave him her heart. Back when she thought they'd always be together.
Now **Hunter** is home and he wants Violet back.

Tell Me To Stay (A Novella)
He devoured her, and she did the same to him.
Until it all fell apart and Sophie ran as far away from **Madox** as she could.

After all, the two of them were never meant to be together?

Second Chance (A Novella)
No one knows what happened the night that forced them apart. No one can ever know.
But the moment **Nathan** locks his light blue eyes on Harlow again, she is ruined.
She never stood a chance.

Burned Promises (A Novella)
Derek made her a promise. And then he broke it.
That's what happens with your first love.
But Emma didn't expect for Derek to fall back into her life and for her to fall back into his bed.

Valetti Crime Family Series:
A HOT mafia series to sink your teeth into.

Dirty Dom
Becca came to pay off a debt, but **Dominic Valetti** wanted more.
So he did what he's always done, and took what he wanted.

His Hostage
Elle finds herself in the wrong place at the wrong time.
The mafia doesn't let witnesses simply walk away.
Regret has a name, and it's **Vincent Valetti**.

Rough Touch
Ava is looking for revenge at any cost so long as she can remember the girl she used to be.
But she doesn't expect **Kane** to show up and show her kindness that will break her.

Cuffed Kiss
Tommy Valetti is a thug, a mistake, and everything Tonya needs; the answers to numb the pain of her past.

Bad Boy
Anthony is the hitman for the Valetti familia, and damn good at what he does. They want men to talk, he makes them talk. They want men gone, bang - it's done. It's as simple as that.
Until Catherine.

Those Boys Are Trouble (Valetti Crime Family Collection)

To Be Claimed Saga
A hot tempting series of fated love, lust-filled secrets and the beginnings of an epic war.

Wounded Kiss
Gentle Scars

Collections of shorts and novellas

Don't Let Go
A collection of stories including:
Infatuation
Desires in the Night and Keeping Secrets
Bad Boy Next Door

Kisses and Wishes
A collection of holiday stories including:
One Holiday Wish
Collared for Christmas
Stolen Mistletoe Kisses

All I Want is a Kiss (A Holiday short)
Olivia thought fleeting weekends would be enough and it always was, until the distance threatened to tear her and **Nicholas** apart for good.

Highest Bidder Series:

Bought
Sold
Owned
Given
From USA Today best selling authors, Willow Winters and Lauren Landish, comes a sexy and forbidden series of standalone romances.

Highest Bidder Collection (All four Highest Bidder Novels)

Bad Boy Standalones, cowritten with Lauren Landish:

Inked
Tempted
Mr. CEO
Three novels featuring sexy powerful heroes.
Three romances that are just as swoon-worthy as they
are tempting.

Simply Irresistible (A Bad Boy Collection)

Forsaken, (A Dark Romance cowritten with B. B.
Hamel)
Grace is stolen and gifted to him; Geo a dominating,
brutal and a cold hearted killer.
However, with each gentle touch and act of kindness
that lures her closer to him, Grace is finding it
impossible to remember why she should fight him.

View Willow's entire collection and full reading order
at willowwinterswrites.com/reading-order

Happy reading and best wishes,
Willow xx

ABOUT WILLOW WINTERS

Thank you so much for reading my romances. I'm just a stay at home mom and avid reader turned author and I couldn't be happier.
I hope you love my books as much as I do!

More by W Winters
www.willowwinterswrites.com/books/

Sign up for my Newsletter to get all my romance releases, sales, sneak peeks and a **FREE** Romance, **Burned Promises**

If you prefer *text alerts* so you don't miss any of my new releases, text
US residents: Text WILLOW to 797979
UK residents: Text WWINTERS to 82228